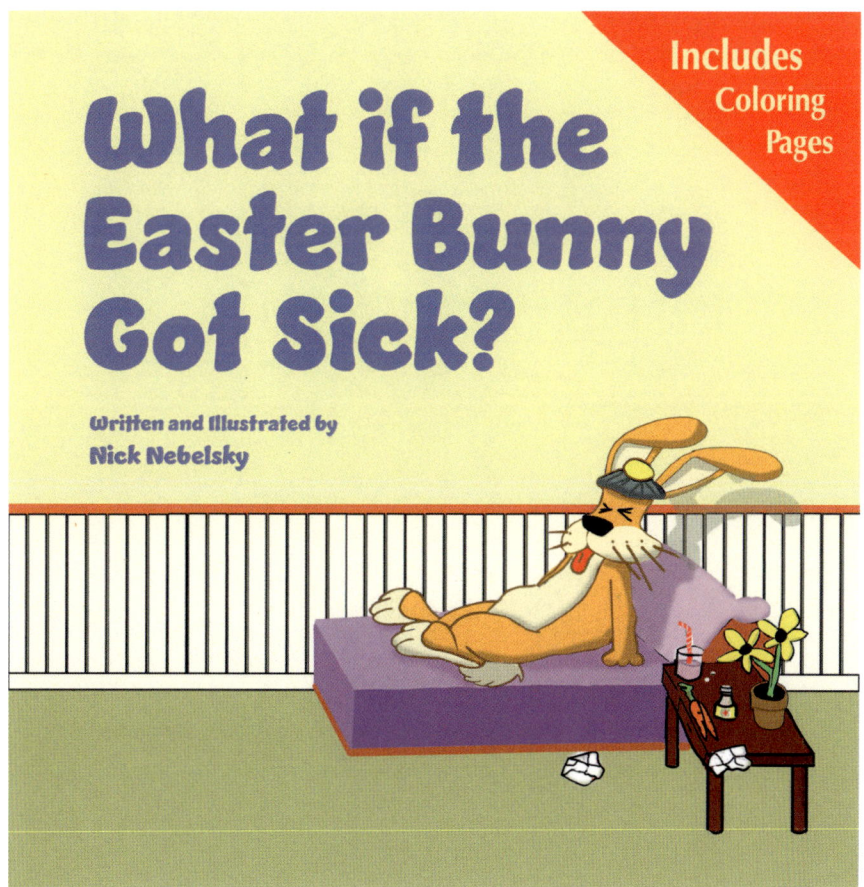

©2018 Intense Media, LLC, Nicholas Nebelsky. All Rights Reserved.
©2013-2017 This book was previously published as an ebook in 2017 and as a mobile app in 2013.

This book may not be copied, produced, stored in a retrieval system, or transmitted in any form or by an means: electronic, mechanical, photocopy, recording, scanning, or other except for brief quotations in critical reviews or articles, without the express written consent and permission of the author or publisher. This includes compact disks, MP3s, podcasts, and all future inventions of media.

Intense Media, LLC
www.intensemedia.com

Printed in the United States of America
First Printing: March, 2018

ISBN 9781980673583

About the Author: Nicholas Nebelsky is a storyteller, writer, cartoonist, illustrator and former greeting card artist. He is also the author and publisher of several other books, apps, and recordings available on Amazon.com, BN.com, and iTunes.

Each year, Lucy Goosey gathers her best eggs and brings them to the Easter Bunny.

At least I think it's a carrot. All I know is he does wonders with eggs. I'm not talking scrambled or fried.

Let's see if he's home.

Lucy is so silly! She believes that if she flaps her wings really hard, an amazing idea will pop out of her head.

Before you could say, "purple, polka-dotted petunias," Lucy Goosey had grabbed the basket of eggs and flown away.

Lucy told all of her friends about how sick the Easter Bunny was. They agreed to do whatever it took to make sure all of the children had Easter Eggs on Easter Sunday!

Her friends painted the eggs as fast as they could. Yet, with just a few days left, Lucy was worried that the eggs wouldn't be done in time for Easter.

The Easter Bunny was sad that he was too sick to help Lucy and the other animals. So he decided that the best thing he could do was to give them a little present with the help of a little magic.

The Easter Bunny opened a secret drawer and inside was a special box filled with magic stardust.

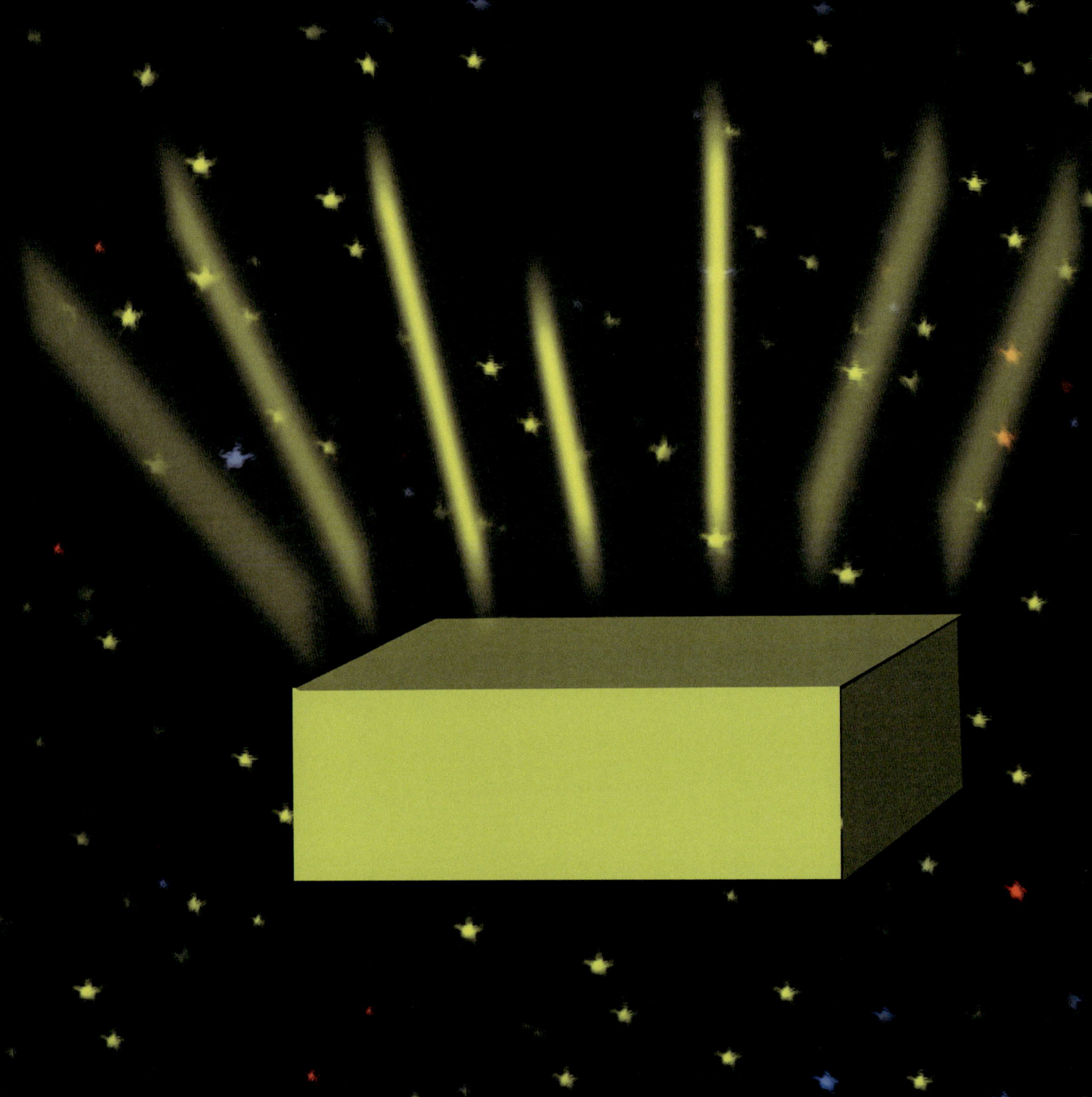

All the Easter eggs were decorated,

but now there was just one small problem . . .

Who was going to deliver them all?

Who were you expecting?

The Easter Bunny?

Happy Easter

from all of us at Stuffed Books

a small division of Intense Media, LLC

Color Some Eggs

Please help the Easter Bunny!

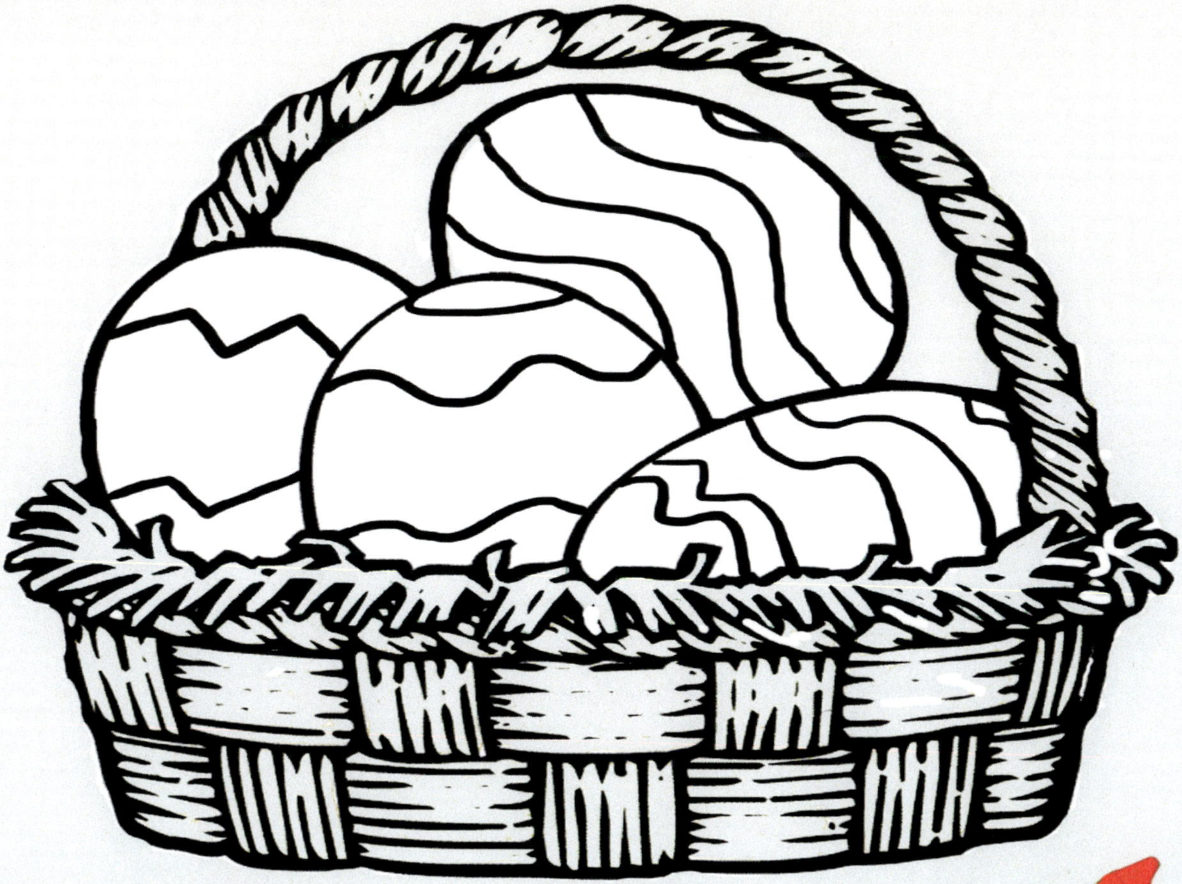

Color Swatches

Share #StuffedBooksEaster

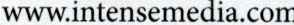

www.intensemedia.com

Color Some Eggs

Color Swatches

Please help the Easter Bunny!

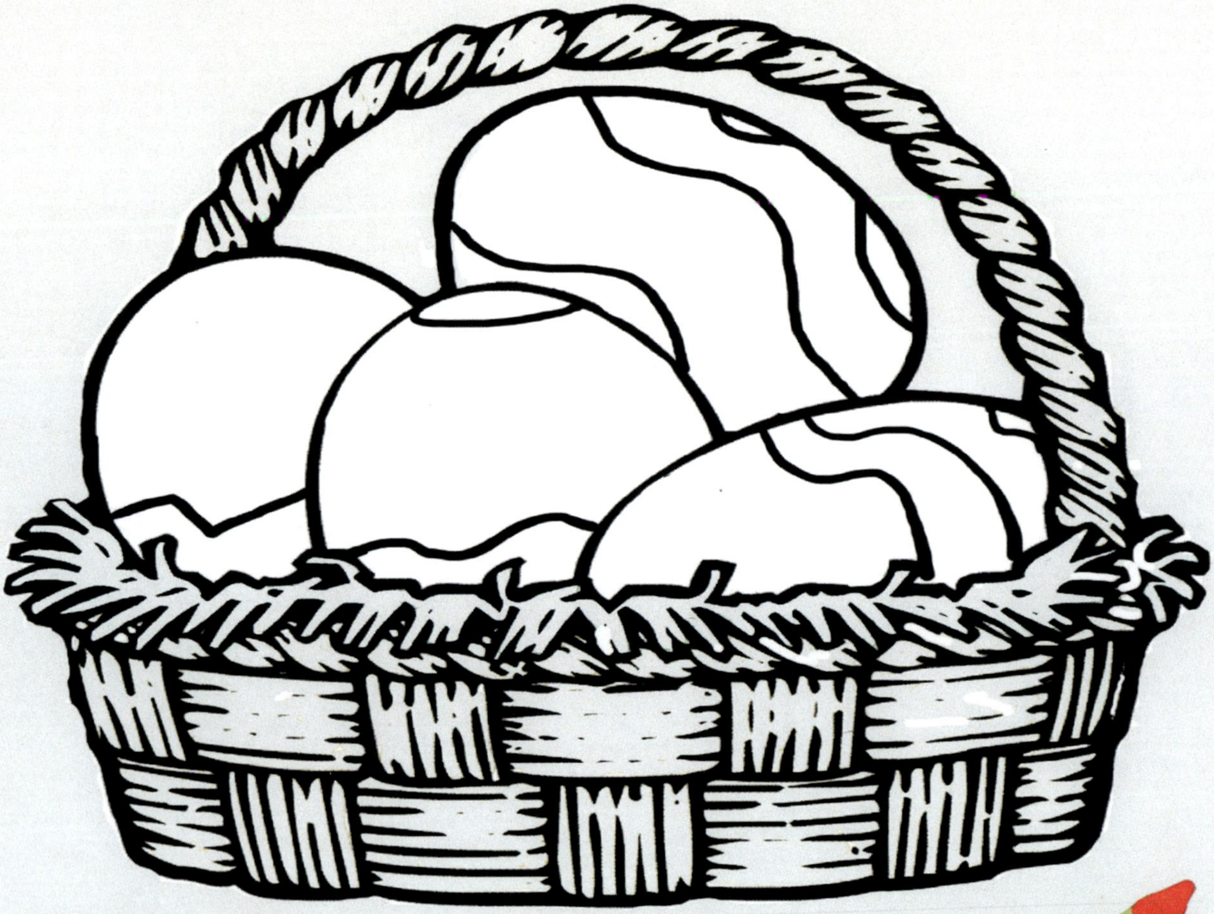

Share #StuffedBooksEaster

 Follow us on Pinterest
 Follow us on Instagram
 Follow us on twitter

www.intensemedia.com

Color Some Eggs

Stuffed Books Color Swatches

Please help the Easter Bunny!

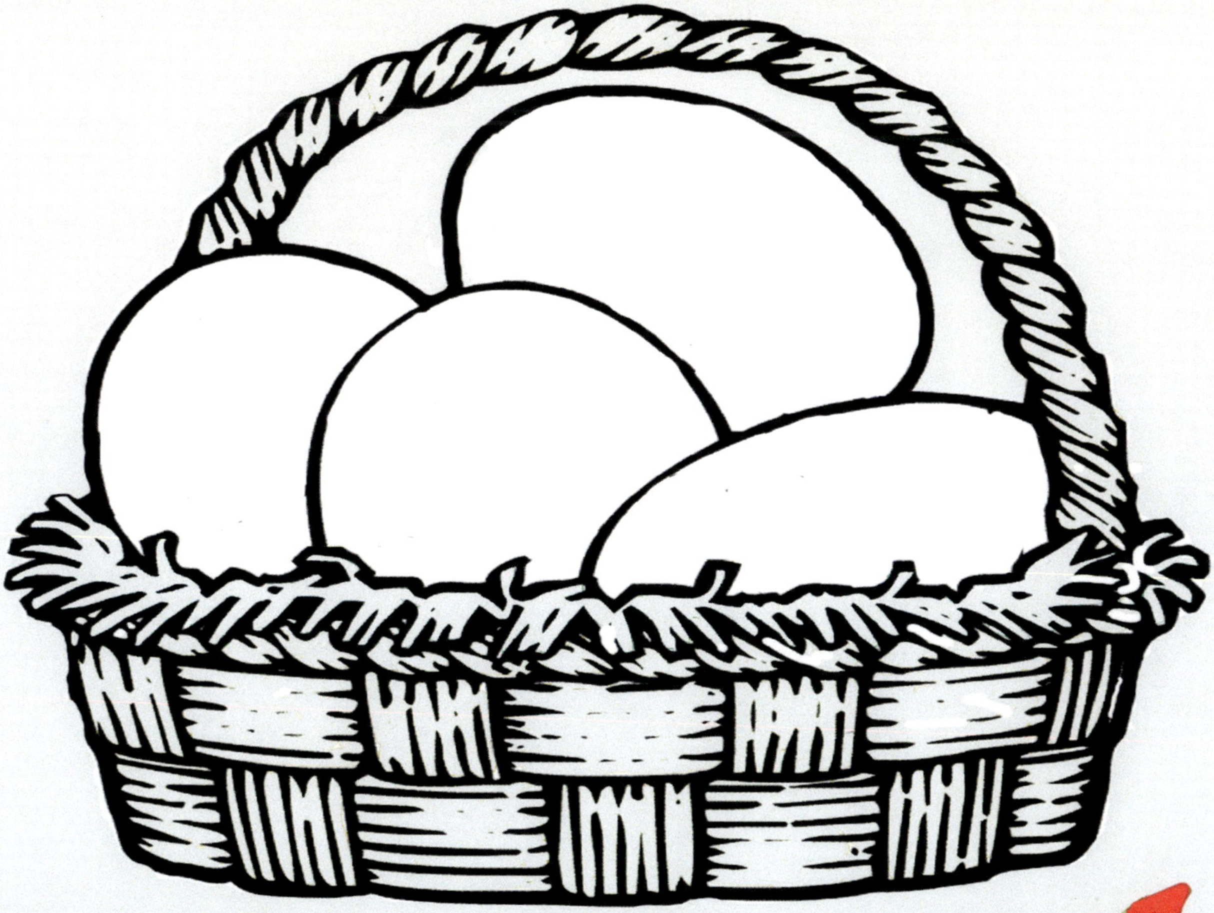

Share #StuffedBooksEaster

www.intensemedia.com

Color Some Eggs

Please help the Easter Bunny!

Color Swatches

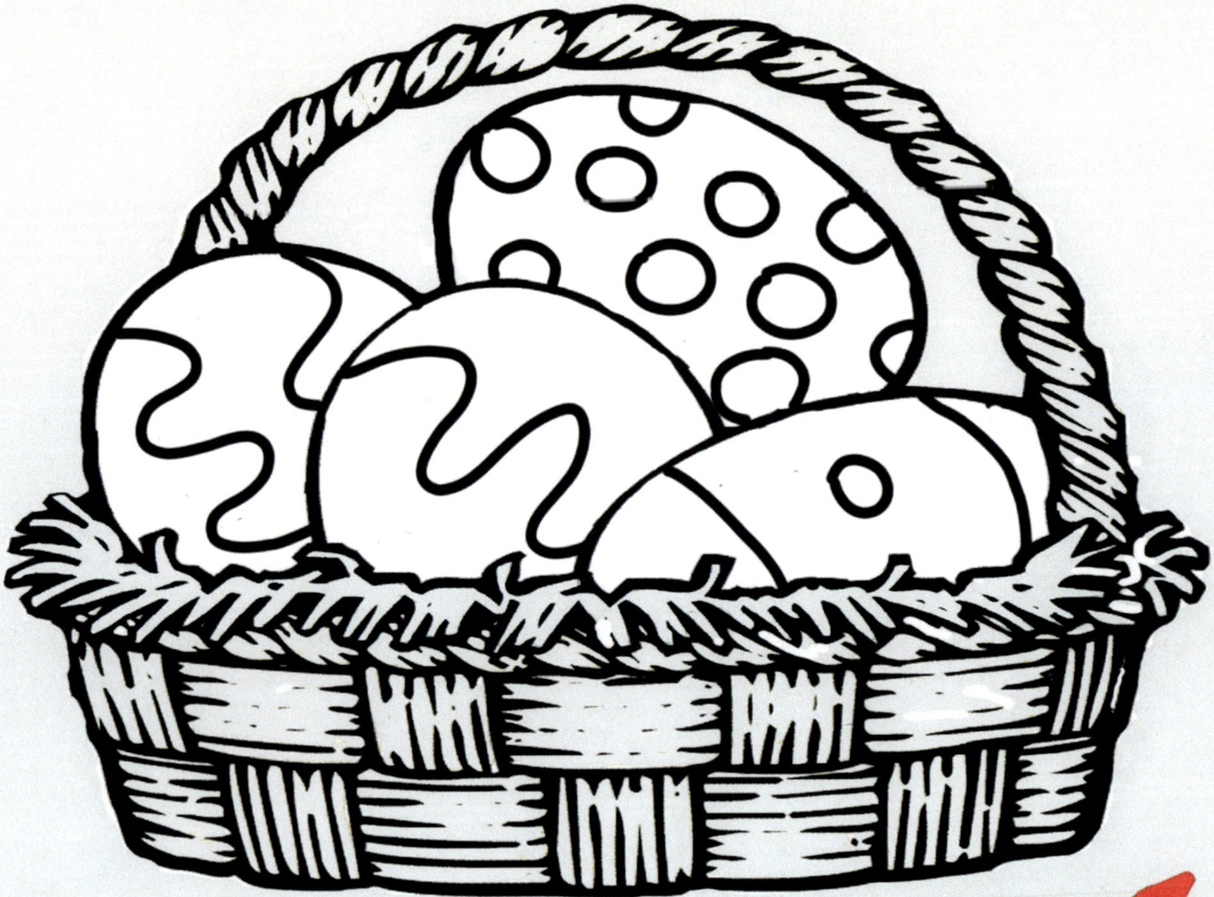

Share #StuffedBooksEaster

www.intensemedia.com

Color Some Eggs

# Color Swatches

Please help the Easter Bunny!

Share #StuffedBooksEaster

www.intensemedia.com

Color Some Eggs

Color Swatches

Please help the Easter Bunny!

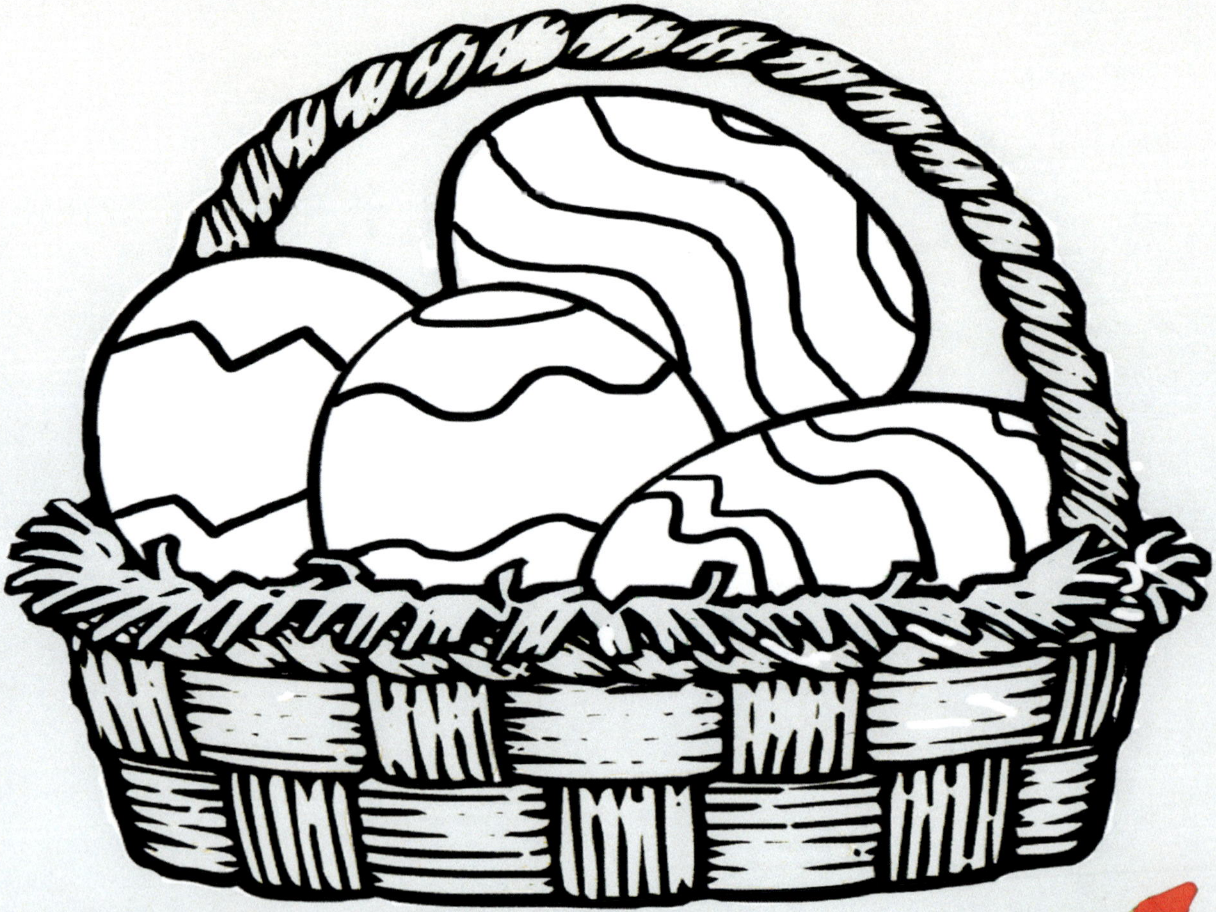

Share #StuffedBooksEaster

www.intensemedia.com

More books from Nicholas Nebelsky (Nick)

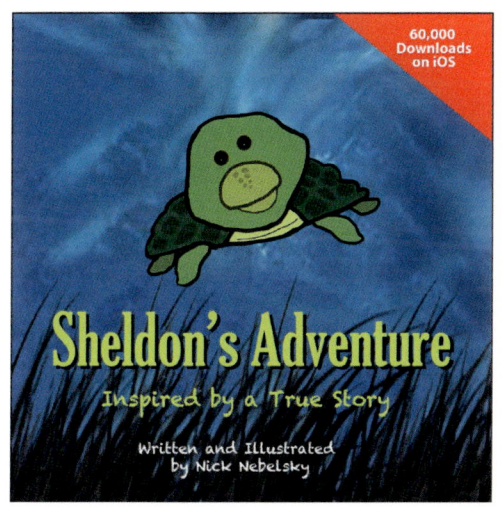
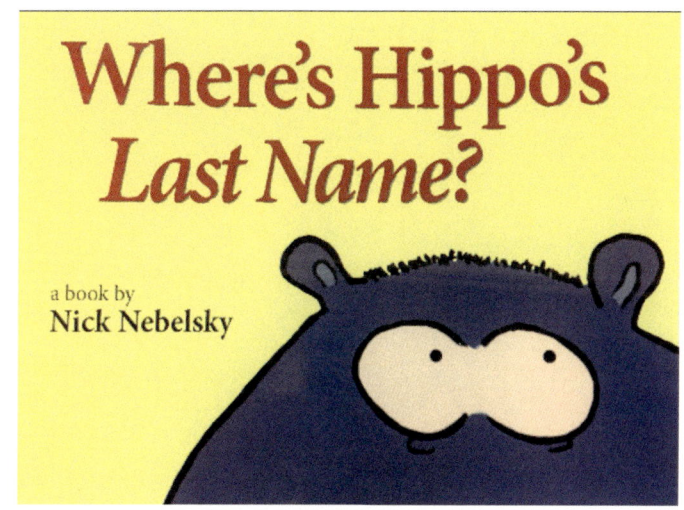

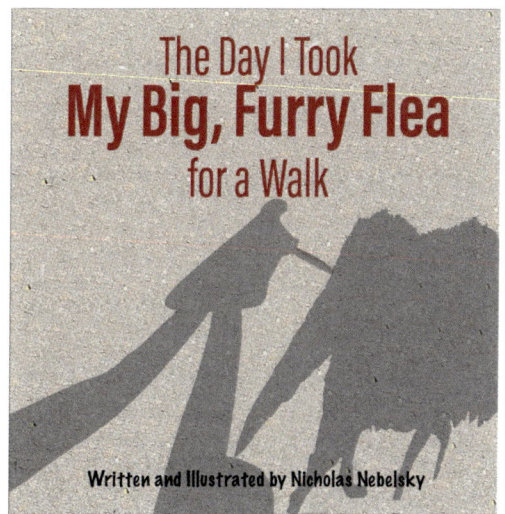

Buy on Amazon.com

Made in the USA
Middletown, DE
26 July 2019